Delicious English
CARAMEL TREE

www.carameltree.com

The Queen
and
Mr. Cunningham

CARAMEL TREE

Chapter 1

Mr. Cunningham's Problem

My cat, Queen Scruffabella,

is starting to remind me of our neighbor, Mr. Cunningham. The Queen is gray and furry; Mr. Cunningham isn't all gray, but his hair is gray, and his arms are furry.

   The Queen has a very loud voice and so does Mr. Cunningham. And now, they both seem to have trouble hearing me.

Mr. Cunningham is always yelling at me from his vegetable garden about something.

"Hey, you!" he'll shout. He always calls me by saying, 'Hey, you!'

"Hi, Mr. Cunningham," I'll answer politely. I'm always very polite when I speak to adults.

Then he'll ask me the same question about sixteen times -- like, "How does your baseball keep getting into my vegetable garden?"

I'll say I'm sorry three or four times, but he can't hear me. Finally, I'll scream,

"Soooorryyyy!" and he'll throw the ball back to me.

Mom says his ears don't work very well. She says we have to be patient with Mr. Cunningham because he is all alone now that his wife died last year.

Mrs. Cunningham never yelled at me. She baked cookies for me, and she even made a green and red cake for us at Christmas time. It was my favorite holiday treat.

I think Mr. Cunningham made himself deaf by blowing on his old bagpipes. Mom says he brought them over with him when he moved here from Scotland. Some nights, I like listening to his music.

Other nights, I wish he would have left those old bagpipes in Scotland!

It doesn't seem fair. He is allowed to yell at me, but I'm not allowed to say anything about his noise.

When I'm watching cartoons on television, I close the door but usually, I can still hear him. Maybe he thinks if he blows hard enough, Mrs.Cunningham will still be able to hear him. When she was healthy, she used to dance to Mr. Cunningham's bagpipe music. I don't think very many people know how to dance like Mrs. Cunningham. I guess, if I miss her, Mr. Cunningham must really miss her...

Chapter 2
A Test for Queen Scruffabella

The Queen is always yelling at me too, just like Mr. Cunningham. Actually, she only meows at me, but she meows very loudly. She meows to get out, then two seconds later, she meows to get back in. **In, out; in, out.** I think she would do that all day if I kept listening to her. She is just never happy.

When she was a kitten, she used to stay outside for hours. Sometimes, she even stayed out overnight.

One time, last summer, she disappeared for three whole days. When she came back, part of her left ear was missing. If the outside of your ear is damaged, does that mean the inside of your ear doesn't work?

Last night, I started thinking

– if both Mr. Cunningham and the Queen are always grouchy and shouting, well, meowing in the Queen's case, maybe she can't hear very well either. So, this morning, I decided to test her.

It is easy to find the Queen because she usually wants to stay inside now. She probably doesn't feel safe because she can't hear dogs tippy-toeing up behind her when she is outside. When she was younger, she used to love climbing trees in the park and sleeping in the grass.

This morning, while she was sleeping by her favorite kitchen window, I snuck up behind her and blew hard on my basketball whistle. Her ears didn't twitch one little bit.

Then I got out the electric can opener and a can of tuna – her favorite treat. My parents got the can opener for a wedding present about a hundred years ago. It makes a lot of noise, like a dentist's drill. The Queen always comes running as soon as she hears that can opener. I turned on the can opener and it made a loud VRRRRR sound, but she kept on snoring. She didn't hear the can opener grinding at all.

It must be true then! The Queen can't hear, just like Mr. Cunningham. They sure have a lot of things in common; they are both gray and furry, they both have loud voices, and now, they both can't hear very well. Hmmmmm...

Aaaachoooo! My baby brother, Lucas, sure sneezes a lot. His nose is as small as a blueberry. How can he have so many sneezes inside such a small nose? He is only two months old, and it seems like he sneezes all the time. I feel sorry for him, but he is only a baby.

He doesn't have to worry about blowing his nose in front of a room full of nine-year-olds. When I have a cold at school, I ask to go to the washroom to blow my nose, so I won't be embarrassed.

One morning, at breakfast, Mom said, "I took your brother to see Dr. Wilson yesterday. Dr. Wilson thinks Lucas might be allergic to the Queen. That could explain why he sneezes so much and why his eyes are red and watery. We may have to find the Queen a new home."

"But, she was here first – she's been here forever!" I argued. "Maybe Lucas should go live somewhere else. The Queen's been in our family even longer than me. Lucas just got here. It's only fair that he should be the one to find a new home."

Mom laughed and shook her head. "The Queen is our pet. Lucas is a person – he is your brother, Liam. Brothers are even more important than pets."

"But he doesn't do anything. He can't even talk," I said. "Why is he more important than the Queen? All Lucas does is cry."

"Someday, Lucas will be able to play with you," Mom said. "My brother is my best friend, and someday Lucas will be your best friend, too."

"But, the Queen is my best friend now. Where would she go to find a new home? She's kind of grouchy, she's really fussy about her food, and she has to have tuna at least once a week. Where would she find a new family that would know how to look after her?" I asked.

"We'll have to think about that," Mom said. "I'm sure we can find a solution to the problem. One way we can find out if Lucas is allergic is to have the Queen take a vacation. If she was away, and Lucas stopped sneezing, that would probably prove he is allergic to cats."

"Where could she go on a vacation? To Grandma's? To the beach? To Wonder World?" I asked.

"Can I go with her?"

"Okay, Liam. Let's think about it tonight, and we'll talk some more tomorrow," Mom said.

Chapter 4

My Brilliant Idea

After Mom ran my bath water, I climbed into the bathtub. I practiced holding my breath underwaterfor a few minutes. Where could the Queen go on a vacation all by herself? Where could she go that she wouldn't be homesick? It would have to be some place where she could visit me because I'm her best friend. I put my head back under the water and blew a few bubbles. It sounded funny and quiet underwater.

After the bubbles stopped, I listened carefully, but I could not hear anything. *'Is this what the world sounds like to a deaf person?'* I would be so lonely if I couldn't hear people talking to me.

I sat back up quickly and smiled. Sometimes, things just fit together – like my hand and Dad's old baseball glove.

"Maybe the Queen could go live with Mr. Cunningham," I said out loud. I jumped up and climbed out of the bathtub.

I dried myself off quickly, then pulled on my

dragon pajamas, and ran into the living room.

"Mr. Cunningham!" I shouted.

"What... where?" Mom said. "Is he at the door?"

"No... the Queen could have her vacation at

Mr. Cunningham's," I said. The Queen purred loudly

and rubbed up against me. "We could see *her* every day, and she could keep *him* company."

Mom smiled. "When did you get to be so smart? That's a brilliant idea, Liam. We'll talk to Mr. Cunningham tomorrow."

Chapter 5
A New Home for the Queen

When I tried to explain about Lucas' cat allergy and the Queen's vacation to Mr. Cunningham, he looked sad. At first, he thought I said the Queen was 'dead.' "Not dead – DEAF," I yelled in his ear. I pulled on my own ears, just in case he still hadn't heard me. "Like you."

He smiled and nodded his head. "I think that would be very nice," he said.

"She complains a little," I said, "but she won't mind you playing the bagpipes because she can't hear very well."

He smiled again and looked at the door. "Did you say something about a bell?" he asked.

I shook my head and grinned. "I'll bring her over tomorrow," I said.

I went home and packed a suitcase for the Queen. She owns a lot of stuff, for a cat.

I filled a grocery bag with all her favorite treats, including her pink dish with the goldfish I painted on it.

After breakfast the next morning, I took her to Mr. Cunningham's house. I don't really think he understood much of what I said, but he looked happy to see the Queen. "She can sleep in Mrs. Cunningham's bed," he said.

"I think Queen Scruffabella would really like that, Mr. Cunningham," I said, "and she likes to be scratched, like this."

"That makes her screech, did you say?"

I smiled and shook my head. "Is it all right if I come visit her sometimes?" I asked.

He just nodded and closed the door.

For the first few days, I missed the
Queen a lot. But after I had visited her a few times,
I knew that she was enjoying her vacation. She didn't
have her own big bed at our house!

So, now it is quieter at our house; there is not as
much sneezing, and not as much meowing. Sometimes,
when I'm in bed on a warm night with the window open,
I can hear them. Old Queen Scruffabella meows right
along with the song *Amazing Grace* on Mr. Cunningham's
bagpipes, and it sure does sound amazing!